Saturday Sancocho

Leyla Torres

A SUNBURST BOOK / FARRAR, STRAUS AND GIROUX

Every Saturday, Maria Lili looked forward to making chicken sancocho with her grandparents Mama Ana and Papa Angelino. Just the thought of stew simmering on the stove and filling the house with the aroma of cilantro made her mouth water. But one Saturday morning Papa Angelino announced, "There is no money for sancocho. Not even a penny to buy the vegetables, let alone a chicken. All we have is a dozen eggs."

"Then we will use the eggs to make sancocho," replied Mama Ana.

"Egg sancocho! Everyone knows sancocho is not prepared with eggs," said Maria Lili.

Smiling, Mama Ana removed her apron and asked Maria Lili to take two baskets and place the eggs in one of them.

"Come, my dear, we are going to the market."

And off they went.

At the market square they walked from stall to stall. First they found Don Eugenio and his son, Sebastian. Mama Ana persuaded Don Eugenio to accept six eggs for a bunch of green plantains. It did not take much bargaining, Sebastian was one of Maria Lili's classmates.

The next stop was the stall of Doña Carmen.
She was not interested in the eggs, but Mama Ana
managed to trade nine plantains for four pounds
of thick cassava.

At first Don Mateo was not in the mood for bartering. It took some time for Mama Ana to convince him to take two pounds of cassava for six ears of corn. She gave him a couple of eggs as well. "So he doesn't pout," Mama Ana whispered, making sure the corn was fresh.

Doña Dolores wanted all the corn for just eight carrots.

"All my corn? No, dear lady, your carrots are not that big," Mama Ana said. Doña Dolores settled for three ears of corn, and agreed that it was a fair exchange.

Under the noonday sun, Mama Ana and Maria Lili traded their remaining eggs for onions and tomatoes; tomatoes for cilantro; cilantro for garlic and garlic for cumin, always keeping some for themselves. But they still needed one more ingredient.

"The chicken. What about the chicken?" asked
Maria Lili. "How are we going to get it?"

"I have an idea," said Mama Ana, wiping her
brow. "Let's divide the vegetables equally
between the two baskets."

Mama Ana offered one of the baskets to Doña Petrona in exchange for a large, red-feathered chicken.

"Impossible," Doña Petrona said, sniffing. "I'll give you this one instead." She showed Mama Ana a smaller one.

"No, it's much too skinny," said Mama Ana, frowning.

They haggled until Mama Ana added two more carrots and some cumin to the basket. Doña Petrona accepted the offer, handing Maria Lili a nice, potbellied chicken. It was not the largest one, but it was good enough for a wholesome stew.

As Mama Ana and Maria Lili were leaving the
marketplace, they passed Don Fernando's stall. He
had always admired Mama Ana's hand-knit bags
and suggested they trade the one Maria Lili was
carrying for one of his wooden ladles. With a wink,
he also handed her a colorful spinning top.

Papa Angelino plucked the chicken while Mama Ana boiled the water and peeled the vegetables. Maria Lili chopped the onions and the cilantro. This was a teary job.

That afternoon, no later than usual, they sat down to enjoy their chicken sancocho. Maria Lili ate slowly, blowing gently on each spoonful. The stew was delicious.

After the meal, her grandparents took their siesta.
Maria Lili had something more important to do.

The main ingredients in sancocho are chicken, beef, or fish, and an assortment of vegetables such as corn, carrots, squash, and potatoes. Though this stew is prepared differently throughout Central and South America, cassava (or *yuca*) and green plantains are always key ingredients. The following recipe, like so many great family secrets, has been handed down from one generation to the next.

Mama Ana's Chicken Sancocho

2 medium onions, chopped
2 cloves garlic, minced
1 1/2 teaspoons salt
1 (3-pound) broiler-fryer chicken, cut into pieces
2 green plantains, peeled and cut into thirds
2 ears corn, husked and cut into fourths
1 large cassava, peeled and cut into large pieces
3 carrots, quartered
1 bunch fresh cilantro, chopped
2 tablespoons vegetable oil
4 small tomatoes, chopped
1 teaspoon cumin
salt and pepper to taste
additional chopped cilantro for garnish

In a 6-quart soup pot combine 2 quarts water, half the onion and garlic, and salt; bring to a boil. Add chicken. Cover and reduce heat; simmer 10 minutes. Add plantains and corn; simmer 5 more minutes. Add cassava, carrots, and cilantro. Let simmer 40 minutes, or until vegetables are tender.

In a skillet, heat oil; add the rest of the garlic and onion. Cook until soft, stirring occasionally. Add tomatoes and cook 2 to 3 minutes. Stir in cumin, salt, and pepper.

Transfer stew to a large serving bowl and spoon tomato mixture over chicken; top with additional chopped cilantro. Serves four.

Remember to have an adult help you in the kitchen.

For my parents, Luis Eduardo and Rosalba

Copyright © 1995 by Leyla Torres
All rights reserved
Distributed in Canada by Douglas & McIntyre Ltd.
Color separations by Hong Kong Scanner Arts
Printed in Singapore
First edition, 1995
Sunburst edition, 1999
7 9 10 8 6

The Library of Congress has catalogued the hardcover edition as follows:

Torres, Leyla.
Saturday sancocho / Leyla Torres.
p.   cm.
Summary: Maria Lili and her grandmother barter a dozen eggs at the market square to get the ingredients
to cook their traditional Saturday chicken sancocho. Includes recipe.
ISBN 0-374-36418-4
[1. Cookery—Fiction.   2. Barter—Fiction.   3. Grandmothers—Fiction.   4. South America—Fiction.]   I. Title.
PZ7.T6457Sat 1995
[E]—dc20   94-31329

Reading Rainbow® is a production of GPN/Nebraska ETV Network and WNED-TV, Buffalo, and is produced by
Lancit Media Entertainment, Ltd., of New York City. *Reading Rainbow*® is a registered trademark of GPN/WNED-TV.